MOUNTAIN MEN

Volume 8

Tales of the Wild West Series

Rick Steber

Illustrations by Don Gray

NOTE
Mountain Men is the eighth book in the
Tales of the Wild West Series.

Mountain Men
Volume 8
Tales of the Wild West Series

Bonanza Publishing
Box 204
Prineville, Oregon 97754

INTRODUCTION

Born into every generation are a few restless souls who long for adventure. In the early 1800s this wild breed became mountain men who headed up the Missouri, crossed the Rockies and continued west, hunting, trapping and exploring as they went.

One mountain man, reflecting the general attitude of the day, wrote, "We found the richest place for beaver we had yet come across, and it took us forty days to clean that section." Valley by valley, stream by stream, the mountain men eliminated the beaver. They reasoned they would never pass that way again and, anyway, why should they leave fur for the competition?

A typical mountain man had grown up in Kentucky, Virginia or Tennessee hunting squirrels, deer, coon and turkey gobblers. When civilization pressed in he escaped, in search of places no white man had been. Where beaver were plentiful and would come easily to his traps. Where there were no property lines. No neighbors. No boundaries. Where he could come and go as he pleased and the world, as far as the eye could see, was his.

The heyday of the mountain men spanned only a few short decades. By the 1840s wagon pioneers were flooding into the West. And the free-roaming mountain men disappeared.

TRAILBLAZER

The typical mountain man was born on a small farm in the east and he wasn't very old before he realized if he stayed where he was, his life was as predictable as the endless string of chores he performed.

In the village near home he listened to stories about trappers who had gone off to the Rocky Mountains, their exploits with bands of roving Indians, grizzly bears and the fortunes they brought back in beaver furs. He dreamed. And one day he kissed his mother and his sisters goodby, shook hands with his father and brothers and walked away. Without turning to wave he disappeared down the path leading to a life of wild adventure.

In St. Louis he signed on to become a company trapper. The company outfitted him and he trapped that first winter in the headwaters of the Missouri, bringing in several thousand dollars worth of furs and being recompensed a couple hundred dollars.

"This is as bad as working on the farm, 'cept I'm in the great outdoors," he told himself. He swore the company would never own him body and soul like it did some of the men. After a few years he became a free trapper, traveling and trapping where he pleased and selling his furs to the highest bidder.

In his wanderings he crossed and recrossed the Rocky Mountains as if they were a low bridge. He plunged into the inhospitable frontier, tracing streams to their source and exploring where no other white man had ever set foot.

It was the farm boy and others like him, living out their dreams, who were the trailblazers who opened the West for all who followed.

INDIAN TRAPPERS

Before the coming of the white man the Indians of North America regularly trapped beaver both for their meat and their dense fur.

They employed several time-tested methods. During warm weather months Indians constructed and employed box traps made from saplings tied together with rawhide. Another way was to destroy a section of a beaver dam beneath the surface. In the hole they set a trap fashioned of long poles pointed on one end. The beaver soon would realize the water level of its pond was dropping and would investigate. Finding the hole it moved into the trap until its head became stuck in the small end of the trap and it drowned.

In winter Indians walked out on the pond ice and made soundings to determine where the beaver had burrowed escape routes. They chopped holes in the ice and pushed their nets to the bottom, effectively covering the runs. On a given signal men began thrusting spears into the pile of sticks that constituted the beavers' lodge. The frantic beaver tried to escape down their runs and the Indians drove them along by pounding on the ice. When a beaver bumped into a net it was quickly hauled to the surface and clubbed to death.

This primitive method was successful, although the number of beaver taken was limited. The animals were able to regenerate themselves within a season or two and for countless centuries their population remained relatively stable.

Then the white man with his steel leg trap took millions of beaver, exporting the hides to Europe. Within a few decades the beaver was nearly exterminated from the streams of the West.

3

GREENHORN

William Cannon was a soldier at a frontier post when he quit to join a group of mountain men heading west.

Cannon was not familiar with the proper way to set a beaver trap. He was a poor shot. But he watched the other men and he practiced. He wanted so to be a mountain man.

One afternoon Cannon left camp on a short hunting expedition. He figured if he could bring in fresh meat the other men would stop teasing him about being a greenhorn. After several hours of wandering in the foothills of the Rockies he had the good fortune to come across a crippled buffalo and was able to kill it. He cut out the tongue and backstrap and rigged a pack to carry the meat using a tumpline like the Canadian brigaders used.

Coming through a narrow ravine he heard the leaves rustle behind him and then a distinctive grunting sound. He wheeled around and there, not more than five paces away, was a grizzly bear. It reared on its hind legs, growled a low throaty growl and showed a mouthful of teeth. Cannon was so close he could smell the bear's bad breath and all in one quick motion he slipped the tumpline, shrugged off the pack and started running.

The bear ignored the pack and chased Cannon. The mountain man reached a tree, threw down his gun and shinnied up as fast as he could. The bear could not follow so it set watch at the base of the tree.

Night drew a curtain of darkness over the land. Cannon stayed in the tree and when morning finally arrived the bear was nowhere in sight. Cannon warily descended. He grabbed his rifle and struck out for camp.

When he was safely in camp one of the mountain men told him, "Well, guess you been initiated proper-like. Any man been chased up a tree by a griz an' stayed there all night, ain't a greenhorn no more."

BLACKBIRD

Blackbird was chief of the Omaha Indians, a tribe living on the upper reaches of the Missouri River. He welcomed the white fur traders and from them gained great wealth and power. One of the traders revealed to Blackbird the secret of arsenic and furnished him with an ample supply of the poison. Soon after the trader departed Blackbird claimed spirits had given him a great supernatural power. He prophesied, to the day, the death of his enemies and if anyone questioned his authority or dared to dispute his command they, too, were stricken and died.

Blackbird did not rule by terror alone, he was also a fierce warrior. He waged bloody wars against his neighbors and his exploits in battle were many. One time, after calling on the spirits to protect him, he alone launched an attack on a Kanza village, firing his rifle as he galloped in a circle around the village. Another time, while pursuing a war party, he discharged his rifle into the tracks and told his followers such action would cripple the fugitives and make it easy to overtake them. He made good on his boast.

In 1802 smallpox, like a wildfire racing across the prairie, spread through the Indian nations. Blackbird was powerless to stop the sickness and two-thirds of the Omahas died. Blackbird himself was struck down and on his deathbed he instructed his remaining warriors to bury him on the high promontory overlooking the Missouri River where he had first seen the fur trappers coming upriver in their canoes.

His war horse was killed and the chief was placed astride it. A mound of rocks and dirt was raised over them. As mountain men continued to travel the river, coming and going to the Rockies and beyond, they always glanced upward at the landmark that held the grim skeletons of Blackbird and his faithful horse.

THE TRAPPER

Washington Irving chronicled the era of the mountain men. His writings portrayed the everyday existence of the trapper and included this description of a trapper's outfit: "A rifle, a pound of powder, four pounds of lead, with a bullet mould, seven traps, an axe, a hatchet, a knife and awl, and camp kettle and two blankets.... He has two or three horses, to carry himself and his baggage and pelts.

"Two trappers commonly go together, for the purpose of mutual assistance and support.... When undertaking any considerable stream, their mode of proceeding is to hide their horses in some lonely glen where they can graze unobserved by the eyes of the Indians. They then build a small hut, dig out a canoe from a cottonwood tree, and in this poke along shore silently in the evening, and set their traps. These they revisit in the same silent way at daybreak. When they take any beaver, they bring it to camp, skin it, stretch the skin on sticks to dry, and feast upon the flesh. The body, hung up before the fire, turns by its own weight, and is roasted in a superior style. The tail is the trapper's tidbit; it is cut off, put on the end of a stick, and toasted, and is considered even a greater dainty than the tongue or the marrow-bone of a buffalo.

"With all their silence and caution, however, the poor trappers cannot always escape their hawk-eyed enemies. Their trail has been discovered, perhaps, and followed up for many a mile; or their smoke has been seen curling up out of the secret glen, or has been scented by the savages, whose sense of smell is almost as acute as that of sight. Sometimes they are pounced upon when in the act of setting their traps; at other times, they are roused from their sleep by the horrid war-whoop; or, perhaps, have a bullet or an arrow whistling about their ears, in the midst of one of their beaver banquets. In this way they are picked off, from time to time, and nothing is known of them, until, perchance, their bones are found bleaching in some lonely ravine, or on the banks of some nameless stream, which from that time on is called after them."

THE DAM BUILDERS

The beaver is one of the few animals capable of altering its environment to suit its needs. It builds dams to create ponds where it can live, protected from its natural enemies.

To build a dam, a beaver cuts down trees with long, curved, orange-colored incisors. The lower and upper teeth overgrow each other so their edges rub together, self-sharpening as they work. A beaver can drop a six-inch birch or aspen in about five minutes. The largest tree ever recorded having been fallen by beavers measured over 100 feet high and was more than five and one-half feet thick on the stump.

The trees are cut into manageable lengths, dragged to the water's edge and towed in the beaver's mouth to the dam site. Sticks are placed parallel to the current and held in place by rocks and interlocking branches. After a framework is complete the beaver fills every crack with mud and chunks of vegetation. Gradually the dam begins to hold water.

In the middle of the pond created by the dam, beavers build a lodge from the same material and by a similar process. Inside the lodge is an above-water chamber where the beaver family lives. Entrances are underwater.

Because beavers do not hibernate they must store a winter's food supply. During warm weather months they gather branches with succulent bark and store them underwater by weighing them down with mud and stones.

As a colony of beavers depletes its food supply they work back farther and farther from the water's edge. Sometimes they bring water closer to the food source by raising the level of the dam but they also are adept at constructing canal systems to float food to the pond.

Indians used to judge the severity of approaching winter by measuring the amount of food the beavers stockpiled. If they amassed a large quantity it meant it was going to be a long winter. And when the wind blew out of the north and cold crept over the land, the beavers remained snug and warm in their lodge on the pond.

ASHLEY AND HENRY

In the spring of 1822 William Ashley and Andrew Henry, partners in a newly-formed fur company, inserted an unusual advertisement in the *Missouri Gazette and Public Advertiser*:

TO ENTERPRISING YOUNG MEN
The subscriber wishes to engage ONE HUNDRED MEN, to ascend the river Missouri to its source, there to be employed for one, two or three years....

Henry was a veteran mountain man and he led the first party of trappers up the Missouri to the confluence with the Yellowstone River. A fort was erected, named Fort Henry, and the men passed the winter trapping the Yellowstone drainage.

Ashley was a businessman and he stayed in St. Louis until the following year when he attempted to take two keelboats upriver to resupply Fort Henry. The party reached the mouth of the Grand River where the Arikara tribe had a large village. Ashley dropped anchor in midstream, talked peace with the Indians and traded rifles, powder and balls for horses.

Ashley planned to depart early the next morning but a storm blew in and they could not travel that day. The friendly demeanor of the Indians disappeared and that night they built a big fire and held a war dance.

At first light the Indians opened fire with their newly acquired rifles and 15 white men were killed. Ashley had no choice but to turn around and head downstream. But he managed to turn the disaster into a triumph of sorts. He gave up trying to resupply the interior posts by waterway and switched to pack animals, allowing faster travel and altering routes if a tribe were on the warpath. This change allowed the trappers to range farther afield and opened up the route that would later become the Oregon Trail.

A WAY OF LIFE

Upon entering the lodge of a friendly Plains Indian, a mountain man was kindly entertained. A buffalo robe was spread before the fire to sit on, the pipe was brought forth and the master of the lodge and his guest smoked while the wives busied themselves putting out a feast of dried meat and pounded corn.

The men took as many wives as they could afford to support. The women were required to perform the chores of the household and in the field. They arranged the lodge, brought in wood for the fire, cooked, jerked venison, buffalo meat and fish, dressed the skins of animals and cultivated a small garden.

While the women worked, the men in camp attended only their weapons and their horses. Their time was spent in the company of other men testing their accuracy with weapons, or their dexterity, agility and strength. When not engaged in games they discussed hunting, fishing, fighting or listened to stories of the past told by the old men. For amusement they gambled and sometimes all their earthly possessions, including wives, would be lost.

It was an insult for a woman to have a man perform menial chores around camp. If a man was seen carrying wood to make the fire the other women would call to his wives, "What is wrong with you that your man should have to make a woman of himself?"

A mountain man usually took an Indian girl to be his wife. In most cases it was a marriage of convenience with the woman required to do the camp chores while he hunted and trapped. And when the mountain man grew tired of the life he might leave his wife and children and return to civilization. Occasionally a mountain man married for love and he stayed with his woman until death parted them.

WHITE WATER

William Ashley informed a group of mountain men, "We don't have enough horses to take all the furs out. Would one of you be interested in investigating the possibility of trying to take a shipment down the river?"

A young trapper named Jim Bridger mulled over the proposition. No man had ever run the treacherous Bighorn Canyon, a place the Indians called "Bad Pass". He spoke up and told Ashley there was only one way to find out if the river was navigable and he volunteered to find out. He built a log raft and shoved off into the quiet current of the Bighorn River.

The languid water soon quickened its pace. Ahead it squeezed into a narrow passage between towering rock walls, the unmistakable roar of rapids drifted upstream and the young man braced himself for a wild ride. Boiling white water lifted the small craft, toyed with it, slammed it against boulders and plunged it into deep, bone-crunching drops. The river cut back on itself in sharp, unexpected turns, sending mountains of water crashing into the unyielding cliffs. Mist hung over the canyon like a heavy cloud and the vertical walls were so tall that sunlight never reached the bottom, keeping the surging rapids in a perpetually gloomy twilight.

To Bridger the ride down the chute of Bighorn Canyon was a blur of charging water, exposed boulders and brightly-colored rock walls. The last rapid finally spit the log raft and the mountain man in soggy buckskins into a quiet pool. Bridger breathed a sigh of relief. He hiked back to camp and informed Ashley that the valuable furs could not be risked in the wild water of Bighorn Canyon.

Rafting the dangerous Bighorn helped establish Jim Bridger's reputation. He went on to become one of the most famous of the mountain men.

BUFFALO

It has been estimated that 70 million buffalo roamed the grasslands of North America before the mountain man arrived.

On their way west the trappers gorged themselves on buffalo meat. They butchered the kills, cooking fresh meat over the fire and cutting and drying into jerky any meat not eaten immediately. There were so many buffalo that sometimes a fat cow might be slaughtered only for the tongue and the remainder left for the wolves.

After the beaver population played out, some of the mountain men doubled back and became buffalo hunters on the plains. The most effective method of killing buffalo was to come in downwind and work within two or three hundred yards of a herd. Crossed sticks were commonly used as gun supports and the rifle of choice was the Sharps, made especially for killing buffalo.

The hunter picked out the leader of the herd and shot him through the lungs rather than the heart because a buffalo shot in the lungs usually stayed with the herd until it died. A heart-shot buffalo might run and spook the herd. As long as a man did not show himself the buffalo usually would not stampede, even after members of the herd began to drop dead around them.

Hunters were judged by the records they set. Tom Nixon is credited with killing 120 buffalo in 40 minutes without moving from his stand. Another hunter killed 79 buffalo with 91 shots. Another killed 54 buffalo with 54 shots.

The shaggy, dark-brown hides were baled and hauled east on the railroads. By the 1880s the great herds were gone and the bleached bones remained as the only physical evidence of the vast numbers of buffalo that had existed. Then a market opened for the bones and homesteaders, Indians and the destitute scoured the plains collecting buffalo bones that were sent in boxcars to eastern factories to be processed into fertilizer and glue.

AFTER THE ATTACK

In 1823 Jedediah Smith led a small band of trappers into the country south of the Yellowstone River. For days they traveled across parched land of prickly pear cactus, short grass and timbered draws.

One evening they were pushing through the timber, leading their horses toward a river to make camp for the night. Smith was in front. Suddenly he heard an ominous growling and grunting in the brush and a she grizzly appeared.

Mountain man Jim Clyman wrote in his journal what happened next. "Smith and the bear met face to face. Grissly did not hesitate a moment but sprung on the capt taking him by the head first. Cutting his head badly. Then he gave him a grab by the middle, fortunately catching the ball pouch and Butcher knife which he broke. Several ribs were broke...."

The trappers fired round after round at the bear. It stopped the mauling and released Smith only after life had left its body. The men rushed to Smith.

Clyman continued, "I asked Capt what was best. He said one or 2 go for water. Said get a needle and thread and sew up the wounds around his head which was bleeding freely. I got a pair of scissors and cut off his hair and then began my first Job of dressing wounds. Upon examination I found the bear had taken nearly all his head in his capcious mouth close to his left eye on one side and clos to his right ear on the other and laid the skull bare to near the crown of the head leaving a white streak whare his teeth passed. One of his ears was torn from his head out to the outer rim.... I told him I could do nothing for his Eare. O you must try to stich up some way or other said he. Then I put in my needle stiching it through and through and over and over laying the lacerated parts togather as nice as I could...."

After Clyman had finished his needlework Smith got to his feet, mounted his horse and rode a mile to camp. For ten days he lay in a tent recuperating. On the eleventh he rose and led his men on into the Badlands.

TRAPPING

A mountain man was constantly on the move searching for new country where the beaver were plentiful.

He traveled along creeks and rivers checking for signs of active beaver colonies, burrows in the banks and fresh cuttings for food and maintaining lodges and dams.

Locating a likely spot, he waded into the ice-cold water and drove a stout pole into the mud. He set the trap by squeezing the clamp spring down and flipping one set of jaws beneath the dog that fit into a notch on the back of the pan. He held the trap in one hand while the other reached to the end of the chain and deftly threaded the end ring over the top of the pole. Carefully he laid the trap on the bottom. Then he baited the set by sticking a fresh-cut willow branch into the mud so that it angled over the trap. He daubed the exposed stick with a little of the "medicine" he kept in a small tightly-stoppered horn or wooden bottle.

The Lewis and Clark journals included the following recipe for making the medicine: "Half a dozen castor glands from beaver, nutmeg, twelve to fifteen cloves, thirty grams of cinnamon, all finely pulverized and stirred well."

A few drops of this bait would attract the attention of any beaver in the area and it would follow the odor to the set. As it stretched to check the bait it lowered its hind feet to the bottom for support. When a foot came in contact with the pan, the jaws snapped shut. Instinctively the beaver would dive for deep water and drown.

When the mountain man checked his traps he would retrieve the beaver he had caught. He would remove the beaver tail. Later he would roast it over the fire for his evening meal. The castor glands were taken to replenish his medicine. The hide was stripped from the carcass and later in camp it was scraped and stretched and laced to a frame made of a willow sapling. The pelts were hung to dry and after the moisture was removed they were compressed into a bale. And the mountain man moved on.

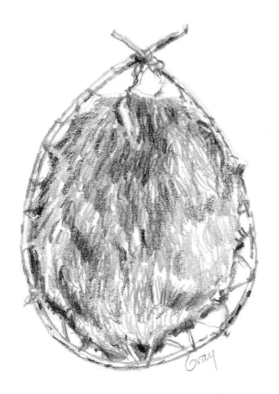

HUNTING

Mountain men lived off the land and took whatever Mother Nature provided.

On the plains buffalo were available in staggering numbers. They moved through the country in long processions. At other times they were found in small groups near water, standing like cattle under a tree or in the water to avoid the flies and the heat of the day. The mountain men, using black powder rifles, easily killed the large animals. They took only the choice cuts, the tongue and backstrap, leaving the bulk of the meat for scavengers.

West of the continental divide, on the open stretches of the high desert, the wandering mountain men subsisted on antelope. The dun-colored animals were wary of danger and at the slightest provocation were given to flight with a burst of speed that defied pursuit.

Usually after running a short distance they suddenly stopped and turned to gaze at the object of their alarm. If not pursued they often returned to the place where they were frightened.

Veteran mountain men used this natural inquisitiveness to their advantage. After jumping an antelope it was customary for the hunter to lie flat in the grass, tie a handkerchief or shirt to the end of his ramrod and wave it gently in the air. The antelope would gaze at this fluttering object and then timidly begin to approach, pausing often and moving around it in a circle that got smaller and smaller.

When the prey finally came within range the mountain man, moving very slowly, would raise his rifle to his shoulder and fire. The antelope would fall victim to its own curiosity.

RUNNING THE GAUNTLET

The Teton band of the Sioux Indian nation were considered the roving pirates of the Missouri. They had acquired firearms through trade with the British which gave them superiority over other tribes in the region. And when the American trappers arrived, the Tetons attempted to stop them.

The fall of 1809 Ramsay Crooks was leading a party of about 40 trappers toward the headwaters of the Missouri River. They reached a point where the river narrowed between high bluffs and it was here that more than 600 warriors let out blood-curdling whoops and ordered the canoes to land on a sandbar down river.

A council was held and the war chief of the Teton Sioux told them, "You go up river, you die."

"We came to see you. We have many goods to trade with you," Crooks informed them. "We will build a fort on this very spot." He ordered his men to begin cutting trees and erecting a trading house. Crooks was so convincing the warriors, after leaving a handful of men to keep watch, departed for their village to collect furs and other trade items.

While some of the men continued to work on the trading post Crooks sent his best hunters and trappers upriver in a canoe, telling them to go beyond the Sioux country and busy themselves collecting pelts. When he judged they were beyond danger all construction work ceased. The Indian guards ventured near. Crooks called out, "Take this message back to your countrymen," and ordered his men, "Shoot to kill."

Crooks and his men managed to outwit the Indians and escape. But ever after, mountain men were forced to run the gauntlet while in the land of the Teton Sioux.

17

OLD MAN'S STORY

Louis LaBonte was an old man when the wagon pioneers flooded into the Willamette Valley of Oregon. Sometimes he would sit in his rocker on the porch of his cabin and spin stories for the pioneer children.

He would tell them, "I come to the mouth of the Columbia River in the employ of John Jacob Astor's Pacific Fur Company. Took an Indian bride, Little Songbird, one of the daughters of Clatsop Chief Cobaway. Moved to the Willamette Valley. Why, I was one of the first farmers west of the Mississippi.

"I've watched Indians hunt deer. See, in the fall of the year, during breeding season, the bucks are on the fight. But wary. In order to get close enough to kill a deer with an arrow, an Indian hunter takes the head and hide of a deer and pulls it over him. He comes in downwind, crawling on all fours, acting as if he's grazing. Occasionally he jerks the head from side to side as if driving away flies.

"Before long the buck spots the intruder and commences stampin' and snortin'. All the while the brave works his way closer and closer. Finally the buck, shaking with excitement, offers a challenge to fight, puts down his head and charges. When he is within maybe 60 feet the hunter throws off his disguise, crouches down and shoots his arrow.

"I've seen what happens when the hunter chances to miss his mark," said LaBonte. He rocks in silence and then finishes his story. "Likely as not the buck continues his charge and gores, tramples and kills the hunter.

"Don't see that kind of thing no more. Nope. Country's gettin' too dang civilized."

LaBonte lived to witness Oregon become the 33rd state admitted to the Union. He died the following year, in 1860, and was buried near his farm.

TRUE MOUNTAIN MAN

In 1830 Jim Bridger and four partners purchased the Rocky Mountain Fur Company. By then the best waters were trapped and stiff competition in the fur business forced the partners to move their operations to the headwaters of the Missouri where the Blackfeet Indians fiercely protected their territory.

One day Bridger was leading a group of trappers when they came upon a large party of Bloods, a branch of the Blackfeet Indians. Bridger sent a delegation forward to council with the sub-chiefs. After a few minutes the chief rode forward and Bridger came out to meet him. In his view the Bloods were treacherous and could never be trusted. Anticipating trouble he cocked his rifle.

The chief rode directly to Bridger and extended his hand in friendship. Suddenly he grabbed the barrel of Bridger's rifle, twisted it and pulled it away. At the same instant two arrows struck Bridger in the back. He spun his horse and amid a shower of arrows and rifle shots he rode furiously back to his men. After a brief skirmish the Indians departed.

The trappers pulled one of the arrows from Bridger's back but they could only remove the shaft from the second arrow. The arrowhead was imbedded in bone and there was no choice but to leave it.

Three years later, during the Green River rendezvous, Bridger asked Dr. Marcus Whitman to remove the arrowhead from his back. The operation, conducted with a butcher knife and without the aid of any pain killer, was ringed with a crowd of trappers and Indians. While Dr. Whitman cut the skin and probed the muscle with a three-inch iron point, Bridger sweated freely and gritted his teeth. He never cried out. He endured the terrible pain like a true mountain man.

CHIEF SMALLPOX

The Pacific Fur Company ship *Tonquin* arrived at the mouth of the Columbia River on March 22, 1811. The crewmen landed and established Fort Astoria, the first American settlement on the Pacific coast; but before the walls of the fort were in place, Captain Thorn announced the *Tonquin* would embark on a trading cruise along the coast. The ship crossed over the bar carrying the majority of the fort's supplies and trade goods, leaving the men on shore nearly defenseless.

When the ship did not return rumors circulated that it had been attacked by natives, the crew massacred and the ship blown up. Duncan McDougal, a partner in the company and commander of Fort Astoria, was greatly dismayed upon discovering the rumors were true. He wondered how his handful of men, cut off from the outside world and surrounded by hostile natives, could survive. At length he formulated an ingenious plan.

Word was sent to the important Indian chiefs along the Columbia River that a great council was to be held. At the meeting the Indians were seated in a circle around a fire. McDougal got to his feet. He thanked them for coming and informed them he knew of the fate of the *Tonquin* and swore vengeance on the guilty.

"White men among you are few in number but mighty in medicine," he told them. He pulled a vial from his pocket and walked slowly around the circle so all could see. "Look at it. I hold smallpox. No harm will come to you unless I draw the cork and unleash the pestilence. Then your tribe shall perish from the face of the earth."

The unfortunate result of this deception was that when the smallpox epidemic did start, the Indians blamed the man they called "Chief Smallpox" for uncorking the vial. Within a few months the native population along the lower Columbia River was devastated by smallpox and 30,000 Indians died.

OZ RUSSELL

Sixteen-year-old Oz Russell left his home in Maine and went to sea, but the confining life of a sailor was not for him. He jumped ship in New York, turned inland and became a free trapper in the Rocky Mountains.

Oz was a mountain man with the rare ability to read and write. He had a special sense of appreciation for the wide-open spaces and the adventuresome life of a trapper. He recorded the events of that age in a book titled, *Journal of a Trapper*.

He wrote of the dangers of his chosen profession saying that the earth would lay as heavy on a king as on a trapper. He speculated that "... my bones may well bleach on the plains like many of my occupation, without a friend to turn even a turf upon them after a hungry wolf has finished his feast."

And he wrote about joining an expedition in Independence, Missouri fitted out for the Rocky Mountains and the mouth of the Columbia River. He worked for this company for 18 months and received $250. During that time he trapped beaver, killed buffalo and grizzly bear and had a running fight with the various Indian tribes of the region. He helped build a trading post at Fort Hall in southeastern Idaho.

Eventually the beaver played out and in 1842 Oz headed for Oregon. He settled on fertile land in the Willamette Valley and became a farmer. He also became involved in politics and served as a member of the governing body overseeing the affairs of the provisional government of Oregon. In 1846 he ran unsuccessfully for governor.

Soon after his defeat he moved to California. It was a bad move. He was taken advantage of in several business dealings and his health began to fail. His last few years were spent suffering with rheumatism and paralysis of the legs. He died in 1892. By then the wild era of the mountain man was only a fading memory.

DANIEL BOONE

Daniel Boone is famous as a frontiersman and as the founder of Kentucky. Few know that in his declining years he became a mountain man.

"Kentucky is too crowded," 65-year-old Daniel told his wife Rebecca in 1799. "I want more elbow room."

They packed their belongings and headed west, settling near the trading post of St. Louis. Daniel used their cabin as a base from which he conducted long hunts and trapping expeditions, traveling up the Missouri and Platte rivers and striking overland into the Rocky Mountains. Sometimes he was in the company of one of his sons or grandsons but most often his black servant Derry, who kept his camp and skinned the animals he shot or trapped, accompanied him.

In 1813 Rebecca died. She had borne their first child when she was only 17 and their tenth when she was well past 40. Through 56 years of wandering she had remained at her husband's side. Now she was gone.

Rebecca was buried on a knoll overlooking the Missouri River. For a time Daniel retreated into a brooding silence but then one day he announced he was going on an expedition. Even though he was 80 years old he spent that winter hunting and trapping in the Yellowstone country, a fantastic land of steaming geysers and spectacular mountains.

In 1819 American artist Chester Harding visited Daniel who was living alone in a log cabin and found him "...engaged in cooking his dinner, lying in his bunk, near the fire, and he had a long strip of venison wound around his ramrod which he was busy turning before a brisk blaze, and using salt and pepper to season his meat...."

A year later, at the age of 86, Daniel died and was buried by the side of his Rebecca. Twenty-five years later, in response to a request from the Kentucky legislature, the remains of both the Boones were moved and re-interred in Kentucky.

RENDEZVOUS

The first rendezvous was held the summer of 1825 when William Ashley met his trappers at Henry's Fork, relieving them of their furs and selling them supplies he had brought from St. Louis.

The next year's rendezvous was held in Willow Valley (near present day Hyrum, Utah) and this time Ashley's pack animals carried wooden kegs of whiskey. The event attracted perhaps a hundred mountain men, their Indian wives and an assortment of Indians and half-breeds. This gathering firmly established the summer rendezvous as a permanent and colorful part of the mountain man's life.

Rendezvous was held every summer until the beaver's decline in the 1840s, and it was noted for its lawlessness. There was constant drinking, dalliances with Indian girls and competition among the men ranging from wrestling matches, shooting contests and tomahawk throwing to swapping tall tales.

Another favorite entertainment was a game called hands. The rules were simple, a pebble was passed from one hand to another and contestants tried to guess which hand held the prize. A gambler stood to lose his horse, traps, guns, even his wife. It was related that one time a trapper wagered his scalp.

An author of that time, George Frederick Ruxton, wrote, "The rendezvous is one continued scene of drunkenness, gambling, and brawling and fighting, as long as money and credit of the trapper lasts. These annual gatherings are often the scene of bloody duels, for over their cups and cards no men are more quarrelsome than your mountaineers. Rifles at twenty paces settle all differences...."

The rendezvous ended when the trappers had spent their year's earnings. Then the outfitter would advance each man a few items of clothing for himself and his Indian wife and equipment and supplies for trapping during the coming season. The mountain men would depart on their solitary ways until the next rendezvous. The outfitter would load his pack animals with bales of furs and if, on the return to St. Louis, he dodged the warring Indians and if the price of furs had remained steady during his absence he would return for another rendezvous.

RUN FOR LIFE

The Blackfoot Indians captured mountain man John Colter on the Jefferson Fork of the Missouri River.

The chief demanded to know, "You run fast?" Colter was well-acquainted with the Blackfoot sport of having captives run for their lives. He thumped his chest and lied, "Me run like turtle. Slow."

Colter was stripped naked and given a quarter-mile head start. It was six miles across the open prairie to the river and Colter ran, dodging this way and that through the rocks and prickly pear cactus, expecting at any moment to feel the biting pain of an arrow or spear in his back. After about three miles the sounds behind were not as loud and he glanced over his shoulder. Runners were scattered out over the plain. The closest, a warrior armed with a spear, was only a hundred yards behind.

Colter ran faster and his exertion caused blood to ooze from his mouth and nose and it streamed down his chest. Over his own gasps for breath he could hear the footsteps behind him. They grew louder. Again he glanced back. The warrior was only a few feet behind. Colter stopped, turned and opened his arms. His action so surprised the warrior that as he tried to stop and throw his spear he tripped and fell. The spear broke in his hand. Colter grabbed the pointed end and killed the Indian.

Reaching the river, Colter jumped in and swam to a pile of driftwood at the head of a small island. He dove underwater and came up in the heart of the natural fortress. He watched through the twisted branches as the Indians searched for him and it was not until after dark that he chanced exposing himself. He swam downstream, came ashore and started running. He ran all night and when day began to break he hid himself in a thicket and slept.

Naked to the burning sun and the freezing nights, his feet cut by sharp rocks and thorns, without weapons, Colter made his way through the hostile wilderness. After several weeks he stumbled into the Missouri Fur Company trading post on a branch of the Yellowstone River, completing what has been called one of the greatest feats in the annals of the West.

TIN BOX

The spring of 1812 a party of mountain men, headed by Robert Stuart, departed from Fort Astoria. Their mission was to carry a tin box of dispatches from the partners at Fort Astoria to John Jacob Astor in New York City.

At the portage around the falls on the lower Columbia River the gleaming tin caught the eye of a group of Wishram Indians. They stole it and the theft touched off a bloody skirmish. An Indian was shot and killed and one of the white men was tomahawked.

The Indians returned to their village where they killed two horses, drank the hot blood to give themselves courage, and painted their bodies bright colors. After dancing to the war song they secreted themselves, 450 strong, on a rock bluff with a commanding view of the river.

Stuart's men were on the alert. They spotted Indians moving on the rock and stopped short. In a show of force they discharged their rifles. Then they waited and before long a canoe approached bearing the war chief of the Wishrams and three of his principal warriors. The chief stood, pounded his chest and made an impassioned speech, calling that the spirit of the Wishram killed in battle cried out for vengeance. Blood for blood, he said, was the principle of Indian honor. Still, he claimed, he wanted to spare unnecessary killing and proposed the white man who had been tomahawked be given up to be sacrificed.

Stuart was very adamant in his reply, "No! Never!" He vowed to fight to the very last man. The chief then hinted the issue could be settled by trade if Stuart made payment of a blanket to cover the dead and some tobacco to be smoked by the living. Stuart accepted the offer.

The tin box was not recovered. Stuart and his men had no reason to continue and returned to Fort Astoria.

COMANCHE ATTACK

On a May morning in 1834 a six-man trapping party headed by Joe Meek and Kit Carson was crossing the high open country between the Arkansas and Cimarron rivers. The trappers were making their way to the annual rendezvous.

A war party of Comanche Indians spotted them and attacked. The Indians, 200 strong, rode spirited horses. For the trappers, mounted on mules, there was no hope of escape. There were no thickets, no outcroppings, no ravines nearby and so the men slid off their mules and formed them into a tight circle. Butcher knives were drawn and the mules' throats were cut while the men held firmly to the reins and directed that in death the mules should maintain the circle.

Blood-curdling screams cut the air and the Indians were almost to the makeshift breastwork when their horses, smelling the fresh blood of the mules, came to an abrupt stop and balked at going further. Shots rang out and three Indians, including the medicine man, fell dead. The trappers had agreed that three men should fire while the others handed their rifles forward and reloaded. The Indians retreated to choose a new medicine man who would lead them into battle.

Again and again the Indians attacked the fortress. Meek said of that day, "The burning sun scorched us to faintness. Our faces were begrimed with powder and dust, our throats parched and tongues swollen with thirst, and our bodies aching from our cramped position...." At length the sun set on that bloody and wearisome day. Forty-two Comanches were killed and more wounded. The living withdrew to mourn over their dead and hold council.

"We each took a blanket and our gun and, bidding a brief adieu to the dead mules and beaver packs, we set out."

The six men moved in a steady dogtrot all through the night. They ran 75 miles before coming to water and another 75 miles before finally arriving at the rendezvous.

TANGLE WITH GRIZ

Early one morning a French-Canadian named Marie and hi apping partner finished checking their trap line and split u o hunt the brushy draw back to camp. Marie walked less than a mile when he stepped into a clearing and saw, only a few feet away, a huge, blond grizzly bear rolling on the ground taking a dust bath. Up came Marie's rifle. Flint sparked and fire belched from the end of the barrel.

Lead bore into muscle and the bear gave a tremendous bellow, laid back its ears and charged. There was no time to reload. Marie turned, desperately looking this way and that for a tree to climb. There were none. He ran downhill and scrambled out onto a beaver dam.

The bear followed. Marie tossed his rifle aside and dove into the icy water. There was one splash and then another and the grizzly came up pawing white froth and swimming toward Marie. Marie dove underwater and swam until forced to the surface. He gulped air and dove again.

And so the deadly game continued for a quarter hour. Then Marie made a mistake even worse than shooting the bear in the first place. While underwater he bumped into the bear, came up face-to-face with it. Its gaping mouth, hideous yellow teeth clamped shut around his head, biting into skin. Pain! To Marie it seemed all time had stopped and the frozen seconds were stretched toward the breaking point.

It was at that point that Marie's trapping partner arrived on the scene. He took careful aim, using a boulder to steady the rifle, and shot and killed the bear. Six days after the mauling, with Marie's condition beginning to improve, another mountain man, Thomas James, visited camp and wrote in his journal that day: "Marie is still in bad shape, with a swelling on his head an inch thick, and his food and drink do gush through the opening under his jaw made by the teeth of his terrible enemy."

MILT SUBLETTE

Milton Sublette got his start as a trapper when he responded to Ashley and Henry's call in 1823.

Three years after his introduction to the wandering life of a trapper, Milt joined Ewing Young for a trapping expedition to the Southwest. After a successful season the mountain men made their way to Santa Fe where the Mexican governor promptly seized the furs.

Milt reasoned they were the ones who had waded the icy streams setting the traps and they were the ones who had dodged the Apaches and Mohaves. He stole back his furs, escaped and continued to trap in defiance of the governor's order.

He was involved in many running battles with the Indians. In one of these his trapping partner Thomas Smith was shot in the leg.

"It's bad," Milt told his friend. "If we leave it be, gangrene is sure to set in. You'll die."

"You can't cut it off," protested Smith.

"Have no choice," Milt told him, pulling his butcher knife from its sheath. While other trappers held Smith down he sawed off the ruined leg. Smith recovered and thereafter went by the name Peg-Leg.

Milt continued his career as a mountain man and in 1830 became one of the principal partners in the Rocky Mountain Fur Company. Four years later, while leading a group of 71 trappers west, Milt had to turn back because of excruciating pain in his foot. Doctors in St. Louis amputated it.

Milt refused to give in to what modern doctors think was cancer. He became an escort for an Oregon-bound group of wagon emigrants but he could not stand the rigors of the trail. When he could no longer ride, a small cart pulled by a team of mules transported him.

He made it as far as Fort Laramie where he died and was buried. He was 37 years old.

JOE MEEK

For eleven long years Joe Meek was a mountain man. After the beaver played out and European fashion turned to silk, Meek knew he could never return to civilization. He headed west, settled in the Willamette Valley of Oregon with his wife and began farming.

After the Whitman massacre in 1847, Meek volunteered to take the news east to the President. He departed from Oregon City and crossed the continent on foot, horseback and riverboat. He arrived in the nation's capital in May 1848, unshaven, dirty and clothes in tatters. He marched into the dining room of the Coleman Hotel and demanded, "Fetch me a piece of antelope."

"We do not serve antelope," stuttered the waiter.

"Then bring me beef. Four pounds'll do," instructed Meek.

After dinner Meek told an influential senator, "Tell Jim Polk that Joe Meek wants to see him." When it was suggested that he might want to have a bath, perhaps a shave, and change his clothes before meeting with the President, Meek retorted, "Business now, toilet later."

While in the nation's capital Meek was invited to many social functions and made quite a hit with his rough appearance and uncivilized ways. At one state dinner a society lady inquired if Meek were married.

"Yes, I am," he assured her. "A wife and a parcel of young'ns."

"Oh dear!" exclaimed the woman. "I should think your wife, living way out west, would be so fearful of Indians."

"'Fraid of Indians? Why, Madam," Meek told her, "she is an Indian."

On August 14, 1848 President Polk signed the act organizing the Oregon Territory and he appointed Joe Meek as the first United States marshal.

HORSE THIEVES

The winter of 1823 a small group of trappers led by Jedediah Smith and Tom Fitzpatrick were headed for virgin trapping country west of the Rocky Mountains.

They crossed the continental divide at South Pass as a bitter wind drove blizzard after blizzard at them. Food was scarce and the men fared poorly. They finally came to Green River where beaver were plentiful and the party split up with Smith and his men going one way and Fitzpatrick and his men going the other.

Fitzpatrick's trappers were soon joined by a band of Shoshone Indians who hung around camp and ate leftover beaver meat. One dark night the Indians departed and took the company's horses with them. This put the mountain men in a bad way; a fortune in furs but no way to get them to the summer rendezvous at Henry's Fork.

They cached their bales of furs, traps, riding saddles and pack saddles and set out on foot. Several days of walking brought them to a sharp bend in the mountain trail. They rounded it and came face to face with a half-dozen Shoshone Indians riding the stolen horses.

The trappers leveled their rifles at the Indians and the Indians slid to the ground. The mountain men rode while the Indians led the way to their camp where the remainder of the horses, except for one, were claimed at gunpoint.

Fitzpatrick demanded the last horse be produced but the Indians defied him. Suddenly Fitzpatrick pointed to the Indian chief and instructed his men, "Grab 'im. Tie 'im to that thar tree."

Then Fitzpatrick stepped near the Indian. He cocked his flintlock and pointed the open end of the barrel directly at the Indian's head. He threatened that unless the missing horse was immediately produced the chief was going to the happy hunting ground. Within minutes the horse was brought forward and the lead rope given to Fitzpatrick.

The trappers backtracked, uncovered their cache, and proceeded on to the summer rendezvous at Henry's Fork.

CAMPED IN YOSEMITE

Joe Walker was an early-day trapper in the Rocky Mountains. In the 1820s he helped lay out the wagon road that would become the Santa Fe Trail. But he is best known for leading a group of mountain men from Green River all the way to California.

The route they took was easy at first and the food plentiful. But as they approached the Great Salt Lake, buffalo and other game became scarce. They were reduced to eating their horses as they traversed the high desert and struggled over the towering Sierra Nevada mountain range.

They came out of the snowy mountains to overlook a lush, emerald green valley. One of the trappers, Zenas Leonard, wrote in his journal, "many small streams shoot out from under high snow banks, run a short distance in deep chasms, which they have through the ages cut into the rocks, precipitate themselves from one lofty precipice to another, until they are exhausted in rain below." They had discovered the scenic wonders of Yosemite.

To reach the valley floor they were forced to let their gear, horses and themselves over a cliff on ropes. They set camp and some of the men went hunting. They returned with two blacktail deer and a fat black bear. That night they feasted.

They continued west and were soon astonished to discover towering redwood trees reaching 300 feet into the clouds and standing more than 100 feet in circumference. They wandered through these ancient giants until one of the men called attention to a strange rumbling; it sounded almost like the pounding made by a buffalo stampede. He dismounted, put his ear to the ground and exclaimed, "That's the Pacific Ocean!"

Walker and his men spent the winter at the mission of San Juan Bautista. In the spring the Mexican officials tried to entice Walker into staying by offering him 50 square miles of land. But Walker, the wanderer, turned his back on California and returned to the Rocky Mountains. Before he died, in the fall of 1872, he directed his headstone should include the bare statistics and the words, "Camped in Yosemite — November 13, 1833".

GOOD AND BAD

Tom Fitzpatrick tossed dry wood on the fire and the flames snapped back and spit a shower of sparks into the blackness. He settled back and enjoyed the rich aroma of buffalo tongue roasting on a spit. Somewhere in the night a wolf howled and was answered. Tom turned the meat and cleared his throat. He told this story:

"Time I'm rememberin' was spring of the year. Been a hard winter. Band of renegade Indians got 'hold of me an' the only way I escaped was afoot. Now a man don't ever want to be left without his horse but sometimes that sort of thing is unavoidable. Anyway, never found a redskin I couldn't outrun. That's exactly what I done this time, outrun 'em.

"Made my way cross-country. Come to a river pushed out of its banks. Tried to cross. Made it, mind ya, but in the process lost ever'thin' I had, includin' my rifle, powder and grub. 'Bout all I had was my name an' my trusty ol' butcher knife.

"Follered the banks of this river two days, subsistin' on buds, roots an' weeds. The evenin' of the second day was diggin' roots of a swamp plant. Why all of a sudden there comes a low growlin' from behind. They come fast. Wolves! Close fast. So up I jump, climb a tree. Go up fer as I can get.

"The pack of wolves set camp 'neath my tree, commence ta howl away the night. They tear up the ground, gnawin' at the tree so much I fear they might chew it down.

"Sometime 'fore daylight they give up an' move on. But I don't trust 'em and I wait fer it to get good an' light 'fore I come down. When I do ya can bet the family farm, I hightail it out o' there.

"Pretty soon I come to a hill, look down and there is that pack of wolves. An' while I watch they bring down this buffalo cripple. Even though my stomach was a growlin' somethin' fierce I stay put, wait my turn. Them devils eventually eat their fill and go away to lie in the noonday sun. I sneak down and have leftovers."

JIM BECKWOURTH

Jim Beckwourth was the son of a Virginia slave. When he was 12 years old he was sent to Missouri and apprenticed to a blacksmith. But he ran away to join a band of mountain men. He practiced his outdoor skills and in time became a first-rate free trapper. Because of his dark skin the Indians allowed him to go where white men were forbidden. He even lived among the Blackfeet, the most feared tribe in beaver country.

"The chief offered me his daughter," Beckwourth boasted. "But after a few days of marriage I experienced a slight difficulty in my family affairs."

He told about a jubilant war party returning to camp with the bloody scalps of three white trappers. A scalp dance was held and Beckwourth forbade his wife from dancing. She defied him. The trapper lost his temper, waded into the dancers and hit his bride on the head with the side of his ax. "She dropped as if a ball had pierced her heart," he claimed later.

The Blackfeet reacted swiftly, grabbed Beckwourth and placed him on a bonfire. The chief stopped them and spoke, saying, "My daughter disobeyed her husband. Would you not kill your wife if she disobeyed your command?"

The chief gave the mountain man another of his daughters and that night, while snuggling beneath a pile of buffalo robes, Beckwourth was surprised by the return of his first wife. She asked for forgiveness and was taken back. Beckwourth kept both sisters.

The following spring he departed with a large escort of Indians and 39 bales of beaver plew. He sold his fur to William Ashley and sent the Indians home with blankets and trinkets for his wives. He continued on to St. Louis and Eliza, the woman he called "the love of my life".

But Eliza had married another. Beckwourth returned to the mountains and for a time was married to a Crow princess. Later, on a trip to the Southwest, he married a Spanish girl but she ran off and he returned to live with the Crows. It was here the mountain man died, ending a life of adventure and many loves.

THE HUNTER

Lewis and Clark employed mountain man George Drouillard as a hunter for their expedition to the west coast. Captain Lewis wrote of him, "I scarcely know how we should subsist were it not for the exertions of this excellent hunter."

Several times during the journey the expedition ran dangerously low on provisions and each time Drouillard came through. One time he killed six deer. Another time he and a companion killed nine elk and three grizzly bears.

After the expedition was complete Drouillard returned to trapping and eventually joined forces with fur trader Manuel Lisa. On their first trapping foray one of the trappers defected and Drouillard was ordered, "Track him down and fetch him in. Dead or alive."

Drouillard found the trapper and when he tried to escape he was shot to death. Word leaked out about the killing and the following year Drouillard was forced to stand trial in St. Louis for murder. His defense was simple; a trapping and trading expedition into Indian country was much like a military operation and if a man were allowed to desert, his actions could put the remainder of the party at risk. The jury agreed and acquitted him.

Drouillard accompanied Lisa on his second trapping expedition. They ventured up the Jefferson River into the land of the Blackfeet Indians. For mutual protection the 21 trappers traveled together, except for Drouillard who spent his days hunting and trapping alone, coming into camp only in the evening. Lisa warned him his life was in jeopardy but Drouillard's reply was, "I'm too much of an Indian to get caught."

But one day Drouillard did not return to camp. The whole party searched for him and according to their report, "We found him. He had been well-armed with a rifle, pistol, knife, and tomahawk and had put up a good fight. But in the end the Indians mangled him in a horrible manner and hacked his body to pieces."

George Drouillard, the great mountain man who had crossed the continent, who had endured for so long in the mountains, had fought his last battle and had lost.

THE SILVER GOBLET

John Jacob Astor sent a gift of a silver goblet to Alexander McKay, one of the partners in the Pacific Fur Company. But before it reached Fort Astoria McKay was killed by Indians. John Clarke, another of the partners, laid claim to the present.

Everywhere Clarke went the goblet went with him. On a trip up the Columbia River in 1812 Clarke, attempting to impress the Indians at Celilo Falls, made a grand and formal display of opening the case and drinking from the silver goblet. The Indians marveled at the glittering drinking vessel and concluded it must be "great medicine".

The following morning Clarke discovered the case open and the precious relic missing. In a rage he threatened the Indians near camp, "If my goblet is not returned forthwith, I shall discover the culprit responsible and promptly hang him."

By evening it had not been returned and Clarke ordered night sentinels be secretly posted. Near daybreak they captured an Indian, his arms loaded with plunder, trying to sneak from camp. Clarke, presiding as judge and jury, conducted a swift trial. He also accused the Indian of having stolen his silver goblet, a charge the Indian vehemently denied.

"It does not matter," concluded Clarke, "I hold you personally responsible for all spoilations of our camp and hereby sentence you to death."

He ordered a gallows be made from oars arranged in a tripod. While this was being done the other Indians pleaded with Clarke to show mercy. Even Clarke's own men said the sentence was too severe and advised against carrying it out.

"I believe in the doctrine of an eye-for-an-eye. Moreover, I believe in the value of intimidation. These savages will soon see we are serious. Let the sentence be carried out," he spoke. The rope was slipped around the Indian's neck and he was swiftly launched into eternity.

JED SMITH

Jedediah Strong Smith was a big man, standing over six feet tall, and was quiet by nature. He took his religion seriously and carried a Bible in his possibles bag. He did not smoke or drink. He never married. He existed only to be a mountain man. In 1826 he became a partner in the Rocky Mountain Fur Company and led a group of trappers west. They crossed the Great Salt Lake country and blazed a trail to California before turning north toward the Columbia River. On July 14, 1828, as Smith and his party were camped on Smith River (on the Oregon coast), Indians attacked and killed every white man except Smith and three others. The survivors wandered for weeks and, according to one report, when they finally reached Fort Vancouver they were, "bareheaded and barefooted, more nearly dead then alive, they had endured on roots and the creeping things of the forest."

A group of Hudson's Bay Company trappers was organized to punish the Indians. They recovered the expedition's furs and supplies, even Smith's journal. The furs were sold to the Company and Smith and his party continued east to St. Louis.

Smith planned to stay in St. Louis and take time to have his journals and maps published, but when he was asked to lead a trading expedition to Santa Fe and the Mexican provinces he agreed to go. It was here, in the Southwest's Cimarron country, that the exciting life of 32-year-old Jed Smith came to an end. He was surprised at a desert waterhole by a band of Comanche Indians and was killed.

In his wanderings Jed Smith had been the first American to reach California overland, the first to traverse the length of California and Oregon by land, the first to cross the rugged Sierra Nevada mountain range and the first to explore the Great Basin. And of the 32 men who had shared his adventures, 25 died at the hands of the Indians.

GRIZZLY B'AR

John Day was a veteran trapper and fur trader. One day in the Rocky Mountains he was deer hunting in the company of a young Pacific Fur Company clerk. The trail they followed was overgrown by underbrush. They kept their rifles at ready. If they did see a deer it would have to be a quick shot.

Ahead was movement. They froze. A silver-tipped grizzly bear suddenly emerged and stood in the middle of the trail, its beady black eyes squinting hard at the frozen forms of the two men. A fickle current of wind brought the odor of man to the bear and he wrinkled his nose at the strong scent and snorted to show his displeasure. He rose up on his hind legs and stood, looking as if he were ten feet tall.

For a few long seconds the adversaries faced each other and then the young clerk's nerves got the best of him and he started to take a step back. As he did he brought his rifle up to his shoulder. John Day grabbed the clerk's arm and held him in a vise-like grip, admonishing in a quick whisper, "For God's sakes, don't move."

The two remained motionless. Seconds warped and stretched into minutes. At long last the grizzly lowered himself on his forepaws and began to withdraw. He went a few paces and repeated his menacing gestures. Day's hand remained on the arm of his young companion and he pressed firmly and repeated, "Don't move! Keep quiet!"

Eventually the bear retreated to perhaps twenty paces before rearing a third time. John Day let out an exasperated sigh, threw his rifle to his shoulder, drew a quick bead and fired. The bear let out a painful roar. It tore at its chest where the bullet had entered, rolled around on the ground and charged off into the thick tangle of underbrush.

The clerk stuttered, "W-w-why'd you go an' d-d-do that? Y-y-you said to stay quiet. Y-y-you said not to move."

John Day dryly told him, "'Nough's enough. I ain't agonna put up with too much, even from a grizzly b'ar."

HUGH GLASS

It is believed Hugh Glass was once a pirate on the Spanish Main, that he jumped ship, traveled overland and lived with the Pawnee Indians. He made his way to St. Louis and joined Ashley and Henry in 1823 on their second trapping expedition.

Glass was older than most of the mountain men, already in his 40s, but he was a skilled outdoorsman and dependable in times of trouble. On his first trip into the mountains Glass was mauled by a grizzly and there was little his companions could do for him except to make him comfortable. They waited for him to die. Glass hung on. After a few days Andrew Henry ordered the camp moved. Glass was carried on a litter.

"He's gonna die. We all know that," Henry told his men. "If we stay with him we eat into our fall trapping season. And we can't just leave him. I'm asking for volunteers. I need two men who will stay with him until he dies, give him a decent burial and then catch up to us."

Two men volunteered, young Jim Bridger and a man named Fitzgerald. The trapping party left the two behind with Glass. After a few days Fitzgerald grew restless and talked Bridger into abandoning Glass to his certain fate.

After they departed Glass began crawling. He pulled his bleeding body over the rocks and through prickly pear cactus. He drank from streams he found and dug roots and picked berries. Slowly he began to regain his strength. After a long time he was able to pull himself up and with the aid of a cane he began to walk.

Glass made his way to Fort Henry where he confronted Bridger. He allowed Bridger to live because he was just a boy and went after Fitzgerald. He tracked him to Council Bluffs and learned he had joined the army. He challenged Fitzgerald but the man would not fight him and Glass coldly refused to kill a United States soldier.

Glass returned to trapping. He was working a tributary of the Yellowstone River when he was attacked by Indians. His luck ran out and he was killed in battle.

THE BEAVER

The history of the beaver dates back millions of years. Fossilized bones of Ice Age beaver, larger than our black bear, have been unearthed. This giant fed on grass and marsh plants but died out at least 10,000 years ago and the smaller, modern beaver evolved.

The beaver is perfectly suited for life in the water. It has webbed hind feet and powerful hips, a flat tail it uses both as a paddle and a rudder, and a tear-shaped body covered with protective fur. Even in cold water the beaver keeps warm. It secretes oil for waterproofing its coat and long guard hairs flatten when wet to shield a dense layer of insulated underfur.

Before diving the beaver gulps air, inflating its lungs. It is also equipped with a large liver that stores highly oxygenated blood. When submerging the blood pressure drops and the blood supply to the muscles slows, but the flow of blood to the brain actually increases. A transparent membrane covers and protects its eyes. The ears and nose are equipped with valves that automatically close. These adaptations allow the beaver to stay underwater for up to fifteen minutes before resurfacing for air.

The natural enemies of the beaver include wolves, coyotes, bears, bobcats and foxes. Otters and great horned owls prey on the young, called kits. The Indians hunted beaver for food and fur but their primitive methods did not affect the beaver population. Then came the white men with steel leghold traps.

The attitude of the mountain men was to kill every beaver they could find and they effectively wiped out the beaver population, estimated to have been between 100 and 400 million. Not until protective laws were introduced in the 20th century has the beaver begun to multiply.

JOHN WORK

John Work came west in 1823 to trap with the Hudson's Bay Company. Seven years later he was promoted to chief trader, succeeding Peter Skene Ogden as head of the Snake country trapping expeditions.

That fall Work led an expedition as far south as the Great Salt Lake divide. Wild game became scarce and one by one the horses were killed and eaten. Returning to the Columbia River, Work wrote in his journal, "We traveled better than 2,000 miles ... and the scarcity of beaver we have very little for the labor and trouble which we experienced. Total loss of horses, 82...."

A few weeks later Work noted, "I am tired of the cursed country and becoming more dissatisfied every day; things don't go fair, I don't think I shall remain long...."

But that fall Work was leading more than a hundred trappers and their families on a trapping expedition to the Sacramento Valley. On the return leg many of the party, including Work, became sick with what was referred to as "hot fever and shaking fits." After their return to Fort Vancouver Work spent several months recuperating.

Work led one more trapping expedition before being appointed the head of Company shipping on the Columbia. After three years he accepted the assignment to command Fort Simpson.

In 1861 John Tod wrote to Edward Ermatinger about their mutual friend John Work, stating, "You will be sorry to hear of the long protracted suffering of our friend Work — he has scarcely been out of bed for the past two months — his complaint is a relapse of fever and ague with which he was attacked 27 years ago.... When I left him to write this letter, upon mentioning your name, the poor sufferer struggled hard to get up — 'Yes do write him,' said he, 'and tell him, oh tell him that I shall never again see him in this world.'"

Two days before Christmas Tod wrote, "I have just returned from the house of mourning where lays the body of our departed friend Work."

MEMORIES

Jim Clyman was a restless young man. In 1823 he joined William Ashley's outfit and went off to trap beaver in the Rocky Mountains. The following summer Clyman became separated from his fellow trappers and, fearing they had been killed by Indians, he turned eastward toward Fort Atkinson, 600 miles away. He subsisted on buffalo. At each kill he camped for several days, feasting and jerking the meat.

He ran out of ammunition and one time was forced to run down a badger and club it to death with a bone. A few days later he was captured by Indians and when one of them made slashing motions at him with a knife, Clyman tore open his shirt and bared his chest. This display of courage impressed the Indians and they released him.

For 80 long days he wandered the barren plains. He described that last day in his journal, writing, "I walked for some time with my head down. When raising my eyes, with great surprise, I saw the Stars and Stripes waving over the Fort. I swoned emmediately. How long I lay unconcious I do not know. The stars and stripes came so unexpected that I was completly overcome... I sat there contemplating the scene. I made several attemps to raise but as often fell back for the want of strength to stand. After some minnites I began to breathe easier but certainly no man ever enjoyed the sight of our flag better than I did. I walked on down to the fort...."

Clyman remained a free trapper and was often in the company of other famous mountain men like Jed Smith, Jim Bridger and Broken Hand Fitzpatrick. After the beaver were gone he guided emigrants over the Oregon Trail. On a wagon train in 1848 he met a girl, Hannah McCombs. They fell in love, married and settled on a farm near Nampa, California.

Until his death in 1881 at the age of 90, Clyman worked trimming fruit trees, cutting hay and tending a large band of sheep. Occasionally he would take down his long rifle and hike into the nearby hills hunting small game, or perhaps only chasing fading memories of days gone by.

PETER SKENE OGDEN

Peter Skene Ogden was 16 years old when he signed on with the North West Company. He came to the Columbia district in 1818 and after the North West Company merged with the Hudson's Bay Company, Ogden was placed in charge of the fur brigades.

A few days before Christmas 1824, Ogden departed on his first expedition from Flathead Post on the Bull River. He led a force that included 372 horses and 71 men carrying 80 guns and a total of 364 beaver traps.

Ogden led five trapping expeditions and often the trappers endured terrible hardships. One time on the Raft River Ogden noted in his journal, "Many of the men came in, almost froze, naked as the greater part are, and destitute of shoes, it is surprising not a murmur or complaint do I hear. Two-thirds without a blanket or any shelter, and have been so for the last six-months."

In addition to his mountain man days Ogden is also well-known for the actions he took after Indians attacked the Whitman Mission on November 29, 1847 and massacred 14 people, including Doctor and Narcissa Whitman. Fifty-three women and children were taken prisoner.

Upon hearing of the tragedy Ogden and a small party traveled upriver. They reached Fort Walla Walla and Ogden called a council with the Indians. He informed them if they continued the war all Indians in the land would be exterminated. He offered to ransom the captives and their release was arranged after payment of $400 worth of blankets, shirts, tobacco, guns and ammunition. Eventually five Indians were arrested and stood trial at Oregon City for their part in the massacre. They were convicted and hanged.

PUTRIFIED

Moses "Black" Harris was a mountain man and a teller of tall tales. One time after returning to St. Louis, he had the following dinner conversation with a young lady seated at his table.

"Mr. Harris," said the lady, "I understand you are, indeed, quite a traveler."

"I'm a trapper, Ma'am, an' a mountain man," boasted Black Harris.

"Well, I bet you have seen a lot of sights in your wanderings," stated the lady.

"Sights? More'n a coon goes over in a hun'red lifetimes. Trapped beaver on the Platte, Arkansas, Missoura clear to the Yaller Stone, trapped the Columbia, Lewis Fork, Green River. Fought Injuns, too. Blackfoot. Damn bad Injuns they're. 'Pache. 'Rapaho. Raised hair of more'n one. In my time done 'er all. Wagh, I seen heav'n an' I seen hell. Fact is, I seen a putrefied forest."

"A what?" asked the astonished lady.

"Putrefied forest, Ma'am, sure as my rife's got hind sights and shoots center. Black Hill country. Deada winter. Come inta this valley'n everthin's green. Green grass, green trees, green leaves. It was all turned ta stone. Putrified, don't ya know."

The woman looked at him skeptically but Black Harris ignored her, and continued, "I heerd this bird singin' an' I up an' shoot 'im. His head broke off an' rolls on the ground. But the singin' never stops. Just keeps goin'."

"Mr. Harris, how could that be?" the woman wanted to know. "How could the bird's singing continue after you had shot off his head?"

"Easy, Ma'am, " Black Harris told her dryly. "The song, why it were putrified, too."

47

WHITE HAIR

The 1832 summer rendezvous was to be held in Pierre's Hole. Several fur companies were trying to get there first in the hope of skimming the best furs.

Thomas "Broken Hand" Fitzpatrick, leader of the Rocky Mountain Fur Company, decided to leave his supply train in charge of Bill Sublette. He took a fast horse and galloped west to tell the trappers it was on the way.

One afternoon, four days after leaving the supply train, Fitzpatrick was sitting on a boulder gnawing on a piece of jerky while his horse grazed. He heard a noise behind him, turned and found himself face to face with a grizzly.

Fitzpatrick recalled, "After discovering I was in no ways bashful, that griz bowed, turned and ran — I did the same." The bear looked back and saw the mountain man running so he wheeled and gave chase. Just as Fitzpatrick reached his horse it shied and ran away. Again Fitzpatrick confronted the grizzly. Once more it turned away; it went back to the boulder, found the chunk of jerky and began eating. Fitzpatrick recalled, "I crept to my gun, took deliberate aim and killed him on the spot."

The next day Fitzpatrick met with more adventure. He was attacked by Indians and chased onto a rocky hillside. He abandoned his horse and, finding a crevice between rocks, he slipped inside and stuffed the opening with leaves. Here he remained for several days without blankets or provisions.

The Indians continued to search for Fitzpatrick but he was able to escape and made his way down the Green River valley toward the rendezvous. He traveled at night and subsisted on roots and leaves.

The supply train arrived at the rendezvous and Sublette and the others were concerned that Fitzpatrick was missing. They were arranging a search party when Fitzpatrick stumbled into camp. He was dazed and hungry, his buckskins were torn and his feet were bleeding. But the most noticeable difference was that during his ordeal his hair had turned snow-white. From that day forward Thomas "Broken Hand" Fitzpatrick was known as "White Hair".

KIT CARSON

Kit Carson was small in stature, standing only five feet four inches and weighing 125 pounds; but he was tall in courage. As a 16-year-old he ran away from home to join trapper Ewing Young. They traveled and trapped through the Southwest and into southern California. After that Carson signed on with Tom Fitzpatrick in the Rocky Mountains. It was here, while at rendezvous on the Green River, that Carson displayed his raw courage.

A French-Canadian named Shunar attended the rendezvous and according to Carson, "Shunar was a giant of a man, a loudmouth bully, who made a practice of whipping every man he was displeased with — and that was nearly all. One day after whipping several men he announced whipping Americans was like taking a switch to children."

Carson marched up to Shunar and without mincing words announced, "I do not like such talk from any man. If you keep on talking that way I'll rip out your guts."

Shunar said not a word as he wheeled, jumped on the back of his horse and rode into the meadow in front of the camp.

"I grabbed the first arms I could get hold of, my pistol, mounted and galloped out to meet the challenge," Carson told. "Am I the one you're fixin' to shoot?" he growled to Shunar.

Shunar shook his shaggy head but at the same time he was drawing his long rifle. Two shots rang out so close together bystanders swore there was only one. Shunar, shot through his hand, went over backwards off his horse. Carson claimed Shunar's ball "...passed my head, cutting my hair and the powder burned my eyes."

There are conflicting reports of what happened next. Some say Carson finished the job while others say Shunar begged for his life and was allowed to leave camp.

The exploits of Kit Carson might never have come to the public's attention had it not been for a chance meeting aboard a Missouri River steamboat with John C. Fremont. Fremont hired Carson as a guide and wrote glowing reports about his prowess in the wilderness.

Carson's exploits were recorded in a series of dime novels and he became a legend in his own time. He died at age 58, in 1868, as a national hero.

THE WAY OF THE TRAPPER

The inventor of the steel leg-hold trap is unknown but historians believe the device may date back to the 1400s. European immigrants brought the first traps to North America.

The typical beaver trap weighed three and one-half pounds, enough to hold a beaver underwater while it drowned. It had two powerful springs to keep the trap jaws closed so a struggling beaver could not pull its leg free. The trap was attached to a chain which was fastened to an immovable object like a tree root or a shaft driven into the mud.

A mountain man paid about five dollars for each trap and used between six and a dozen on a trap line. The beaver he caught were skinned on the spot and the trapper took not only the fur but the castor gland to use for preparing future trapping bait, and the broad, flat tail. This delicacy was cooked over the camp fire while the trapper tended to the chore of scraping and fleshing the skins and stretching them over frames made from supple willow sticks bent into circles. The skins were set out to dry, flesh side up, in the sun.

When dried, the plews (beaver skins) weighed about one and one-half pounds. They were branded with a mark of personal identification, tied together into bales and transported to a rendezvous where they were sold or traded. A trapper might take a couple hundred beaver in a good season and would receive between four and six dollars for each quality plew.

After selling their furs, replenishing their supplies and enjoying some revelry at the rendezvous the trappers, singly and in pairs, returned to the mountains and their solitary ways.

THE STANDOFF

In 1813 three men from the Pacific Fur Company, Donald McKenzie, Alfred Seton and Joe de la Pierre, were traveling along the Columbia River. They stopped at the village of Wishram and, since the Indians had sometimes been unfriendly in the past, they took no chances and primed their rifles.

As the three men hiked up the winding path they remarked how strange it was that no one came to meet them. Even the dogs, normally very excited, were silent. Suddenly a young boy appeared, pointed toward a lodge and ran away. The men moved as directed. They hesitated at the entrance and then proceeded, stooping to go through the low doorway.

A fire burned at the far end of a dark room that measured about 25 feet long and 20 feet wide. Firelight shined on the chief, a man about 60 years old, and illuminated a room full of warriors squatting on the floor with buffalo robes wrapped around their shoulders. A rush of Indians sealed off the exit behind the white men. The chief motioned for them to sit. They complied.

McKenzie filled his pipe with tobacco, offered it to the chief, saying, "Smoke the pipe of peace with us." But the old man ignored it and instead began talking in a low voice that soon became loud and violent. He chastised the white men for the conduct of all white men who had ever come up or down the river.

While he was engaged in his impassioned address the white men slowly got to their feet and McKenzie raised his rifle so the muzzle pointed directly at the speaker's heart. He cocked the lock. The chief abruptly stopped talking. For a long moment there was not a sound in the room.

The three men broke the standoff and coolly backed toward the exit with their rifles at ready. The Indians parted for them. They emerged from the lodge and, moving quickly, took the path to the river. They jumped in their canoe and hastily departed.

JOHN DAY

John Day was born in Kentucky and became a mountain man in the upper Missouri River country. In 1810 he joined the Astoria expedition marching overland to the mouth of the Columbia River.

Along the way John Day became sick and he and Ramsay Crooks, a friend who refused to leave him, were abandoned along the Snake River. Crooks later wrote of their suffering, "John Day was so weak that when he sat down he could not rise again without help.... We went without food to eat and water to drink. Death seemed inevitable.

"A very large wolf came prowling around our camp and John Day, with great exertion and good luck, shot the ferocious animal dead, and to this fortunate hit I think we owed our lives. The flesh of the wolf we cut up and dried and laid it by for some future emergency, and in the meantime feasted upon the skin; nor did we throw away the bones, but pounded them between stones and made a broth which in our present circumstances we found very good....

"For two months we waundered about; barely sustaining life with our utmost exertion. All this time we kept traveling to and fro, until we happened, by mere chance, to reach the Columbia River.... We proceeded to the falls where there were Indians in considerable numbers.... The Indians closed in upon us, with guns pointed and bows drawn, and by force stripped us of our clothes, ammunition, rifles, knives and everything else, leaving us naked as the day we were born...."

John Day and Ramsay Crooks were rescued by a group of fur traders and taken to Fort Astoria. The following spring John Day joined a group of men making an overland journey to New York. On the way the strain of his experiences the previous year caused him to lose his mind. He tried to kill himself with a pistol but the ball only grazed his scalp. He was placed under guard and was returned to Fort Astoria where he died within a few months.

RATTLESNAKE DEN

One afternoon, after battling head winds on the Columbia River, a group of Pacific Fur Company trappers set camp at the foot of a basalt bluff. After they ate, some of the men stood guard while others stretched out on the ground to sleep. Ross Cox, a company clerk, was the first to notice a rattlesnake slithering across the sand toward a French-Canadian trapper named LaCourse.

The snake settled itself in the thin ribbon of shade made by LaCourse's exposed neck. Cox whispered to one of his companions, "Don't make any sudden movement. There is a rattlesnake at LaCourse's throat."

"What will we do?" questioned the man.

The men talked it over and it was decided that one would approach from one direction, to divert the snake's attention, while the other, armed with a long stick, would slip up from behind. Cox cautioned, "Don't come in too fast. If you do, the snake rattles and LaCourse is a dead man."

LaCourse slept peacefully as the man serving as the diversion moved into place. The snake watched him intently and when he was within ten paces it slowly coiled itself, its head came up and its tongue darted in and out. The man took another step, then another. The poised rattles began to vibrate and at that instant Cox thrust the stick across LaCourse's throat and all in one motion caught the snake and sent it flying. It was quickly clubbed to death.

LaCourse sat upright and demanded to know, "What's going on here?"

A search of the camp area revealed 50 rattlesnakes lying in the shade of rocks and chunks of driftwood. They were quickly dispatched. By then it was too late to change camp sites so the men broke open a bale of tobacco and spread the strong-smelling leaves around the ground to ward off the snakes. That night, remembering what had befallen LaCourse, the trappers slept fitfully.

MOUNTAIN MAN YARNS

"Worst storm I ever was in was back in the middle '20s," claimed famous mountain man Jim Bridger. "At the time I was trappin' in the Great Salt Lake valley. This whoppin' big storm moves in and it snowed and the wind blowed for the best part of two months straight without let-up.

"And then it got cold! Oh, was it cold! In fact, it was so cold there was a buffalo herd I came across that froze to death standin' up. Using my lariat and horse I snaked a lot of them over to the edge of Salt Lake. I was told the Indians in those parts lived for several years off the buffalo meat preserved in the salt brine.

"That was just one of the unusual things I witnessed in my years of wanderin'. Probably the strangest of all was one time in the Yellowstone country. I was huntin' for meat and happened across this granddaddy of a bull elk. Had horns way out to here, he had.

"So I drop to the ground, take steady aim and squeeze the trigger. Ka-blam! Much to my utter and complete amazement, that ol' bull never flinched, never so much as flicked an ear.

"The elk was maybe 40 paces. How could I have missed? Why didn't he move? Only thing I could figure was my rifle misfired and the elk was stone deaf. I gave it another go; reloaded, took steady aim, held my breath and squeezed off. Lo and behold the same result. I shot a third, fourth and nothin'.

"My rifle, always a faithful and trusted companion, had never plugged up before. I absolutely had to have meat. And so, plannin' on usin' my rifle as a club, I charged that critter.

"But before goin' a dozen steps I run smack dab into an invisible wall. After careful inspection I discovered the wall was a mountain of glass. The elk was on the opposite side, fully 20 miles away and the wall was magnifying his image. That's the truth. I swear."

THE RESCUE

Mountain man Jim Pattie arrived in Santa Fe to request the Mexican governor grant him and his men the right to trap the Gila River. The governor listened to Pattie before telling him he was not inclined to issue such a permit but he would think it over and give his decision the following day.

That night news reached Santa Fe that a war party of Comanche Indians had murdered a number of men at isolated ranches and had taken four women as prisoners. One of them was the governor's beautiful daughter, Jacova.

Before sunlight streaked the eastern sky Pattie and his band of mountain men were off to rescue the captives. When they overtook the Indians they found them driving a large herd of stolen sheep and horses; the women, who were naked, were forced to walk in front of the column.

The mountain men made a big circle and lay in wait for the Indians. Pattie wrote in his journal, "Every man was ordered to prime and pick his gun afresh." The plan called for his sharpshooters to kill the Comanches closest to the prisoners, hoping that in the confusion the women could escape.

The Indians came within range and the mountain men fired. Several Indians went down in the initial barrage but while the mountain men were reloading three of the women were speared by the Indians. Only Jacova evaded swift death. She ran, making straight for Pattie. He wrote, "I gallantly covered her nakedness," and then he returned to the battle. At length they succeeded in putting the Indians on the run.

In appreciation for Jacova's safe return, Pattie was granted a trapping permit. And beautiful Jacova thanked and praised the mountain man for his courage and chivalry. She asked him if she could keep the buckskin shirt he had taken off his back and given her. "Please," she said. "That way I will have a remembrance of you to hold for the rest of my life." He gave her the shirt.

OLD JIM BRIDGER

Most mountain men died young. An exception was Jim Bridger. At the age of 45 Bridger bought land in Missouri, took his third wife, a Shoshone chief's daughter, and said he would be happy to live out his days as a farmer. But because of his vast knowledge of the West he was sought out and prevailed upon to guide numerous expeditions of explorers, scientists and pioneers.

The most unusual group Bridger guided was English sportsman Sir George Gore who traveled with an entourage that included 40 servants, cooks, valets, horsemen and dog handlers. His daily routine called for him to rise at mid-morning, soak in a hot bath, have a leisurely breakfast and then go hunting. During the year and a half Gore was guided by Bridger he shot 40 grizzly bear, 2,500 buffalo, and uncounted hundreds of antelope, deer and elk. Eventually the Englishman had his fill of killing North American game and returned home.

Bridger went back to his farm. He lived to see the beaver and the buffalo driven to the brink of extinction and the continent spanned by rail. His health began to fail and his once erect posture became stooped. He shuffled when he walked, feeling his way with a cane, and finally his vision became so blurred he had to be led.

Jim Bridger died in 1881 at the age of 77. He was buried in Kansas City, Missouri. The monument over his grave notes his accomplishments: "Celebrated as a hunter, trapper, fur trader and guide. Discovered Great Salt Lake 1824. The South Pass 1827. Visited Yellowstone Lake and geysers 1830. Founded Ft. Bridger 1843."

The monument has the likeness of the King of the Mountain Men carved into the stone. And, as in life, the eyes face westward.

THE WANDERER

An early-day writer described the typical mountain man: "His skin, from constant exposure, assumes a hue almost as dark as that of the Aborigine. His hair becomes long, coarse, and bushy and loosely dangles upon his shoulders. His head is surmounted by a low crowned wool-hat or rude substitute of his own manufacture. His clothes are of buckskin, gaily fringed at the seams with strings of the same material, cut and made in a fashion peculiar to himself and associates....

"His waist is encircled with a belt of leather, holding encased his butcher knife and pistols — while from his neck is suspended a bullet pouch securely fastened to the belt in front, and beneath the right arm hangs a powder horn, upon the strap of which is affixed his bullet-mold, ballscrew, wiper and awl."

The mountain man's outfit customarily included a saddle horse and a pack horse which carried all his worldly possessions, including the furs as they were accumulated. He ate fresh meat when it was available and subsisted on jerky and pemmican when Mother Nature was not in the giving mood.

He followed the rivers and creeks, trapping beaver as he went from the Little Missouri to the Musselshell and on to the tributaries of the Yellowstone; the Powder, Tongue, Bighorn and Clark's Fork. He moved to snow-fed creeks high in the mountains, crossed over the continental divide and explored south to the Colorado and west to the Salmon, Snake and Columbia rivers.

The mountain man lived without restraints. He fought hostile Indians, counted coup on the grizzly bears, endured extremes in weather and survived terrible accidents. He explored and mapped the unknown reaches of the continent and as he wandered he pushed the border of the United States all the way to the Pacific Ocean.

Rick Steber's Tales of the Wild West Series is available in hardbound books ($14.95) and paperback books ($4.95) featuring illustrations by Don Gray, as well as in audio tapes ($7.95) narrated by Dallas McKennon. Current titles in the series include —

OREGON TRAIL Vol. 1 *
PACIFIC COAST Vol. 2 *
INDIANS Vol. 3 *
COWBOYS Vol. 4 *
WOMEN OF THE WEST Vol. 5 *
CHILDREN'S STORIES Vol. 6 *
LOGGERS Vol. 7 *
MOUNTAIN MEN Vol. 8 *
MINERS Vol. 9 *
GRANDPA'S STORIES Vol. 10
PIONEERS Vol. 11
CAMPFIRE STORIES Vol. 12
TALL TALES Vol. 13
GUNFIGHTERS Vol. 14
GRANDMA'S STORIES Vol. 15
Available on Audio Tape

Other books written by Rick Steber —

ROUNDUP
LAST OF THE PIONEERS
HEARTWOOD
WHERE ROLLS THE OREGON

NEW YORK TO NOME
WILD HORSE RIDER
TRACES
RENDEZVOUS

If unavailable at retailers in your area write directly to the publisher. A catalog is free upon request.

Bonanza Publishing
Box 204
Prineville, Oregon 97754